MY BOOK

Shags
Has a Dream

GYO FUJIKAWA

GROSSET & DUNLAP · PUBLISHERS · NEW YORK

A FILMWAYS COMPANY

Library of Congress Catalog Card Number: 80-83352. ISBN 0-448-11749-5 (Trade Edition); ISBN: 0-448-13653-8 (Library Edition).

One day Shags was out in the woods with Sam and Jenny and Nicholas and Mei Su when he saw Rabbit. And off Shags ran.

"Come back, Shags," Sam yelled. "I wish he wouldn't chase poor Rabbit," Sam thought.

That night after dinner Shags went out
to the garden to bury a tasty new bone,
and Sam came along.

"Shags," Sam said, "it's very mean to
chase animals like Rabbit that are smaller
than you. How would you feel if they were
big and you were small?"

When it was bedtime, Shags stretched out in his favorite spot under Sam's bed, and he closed his eyes.

He was tired, and by the time Sam climbed into bed, Shags was fast asleep.

Shags slept soundly most of the night.
Then a strange thing happened. His good friend
Little Cat came over to play. But Little Cat
wasn't little anymore. Little Cat was BIG cat.

And instead of a soft meow, she let out a great big roar!

Shags was scared!
He ran and he ran!

Then he got another surprise,

and then ANOTHER,

and ANOTHER!

Everything had become very, very large!

"I don't know what's happening,"
Shags thought, "but I don't like it."

And then, who should come along but Rabbit.
Rabbit was enormous — much bigger than Shags.
   "Help!" Shags barked.
   Shags ran away from Rabbit as fast as he could.

Now he was tired and panting and very thirsty.
But his water bowl had grown huge — so huge
that Shags had to climb up the side to drink.

When he got to the top,
Shags lost his balance and fell
into an ocean of water.

The waves were so high that Shags had to swim from
one side of the bowl to the other before he could climb out.

Shags was wet and cold and miserable.
He crawled to a patch of violets and hid
under the leaves.

"I hope nobody finds me here," he thought.

Just then a giant-sized spider
walked past on his eight long
skinny legs. He gave Shags a nasty
look with his beady eyes.

"Gosh!" Shags said to himself.
"Even the spiders are monsters!"

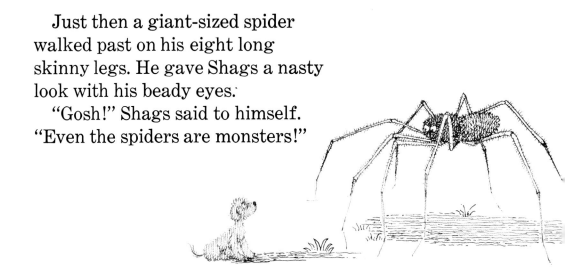

Then a huge mouse scurried by . . .

And a family of ducklings came along quacking
rudely at Shags. They were enormous!

Next, a gigantic frog
croaked loudly at Shags.

And a friendly old turtle
ambled by. Was HE big!

A giant hen headed straight for Shags,
clucking and pecking until he had to
leave his hiding place.
"Okay! Okay!" Shags yelped.
"I'm going! I'm going!"

Suddenly he remembered his bone. "If my bone
has grown, I'd have more of it to chew on!"

Shags raced to where he had buried
his bone and started to dig.
Sure enough, it was HUGE!
Shags opened his mouth as wide
as he could, but he couldn't fit the bone
between his teeth.

Shags was very unhappy. Then he heard
Sam's voice. "Shags! Shags!"

Shags ran to find Sam and then stopped
short. Oh, my! Sam was a giant, too! So were
Jenny and Nicholas and Mei Su!

"Where are you, Shags?" Sam asked.
"I can't see you."
Sam dropped down on his hands and knees.
"Now I see you," he said.
"But, Shags, what happened? You're so small.
Why, you're no bigger than a peanut."
Shags barked a tiny whisper of a bark.

Shags heard Sam calling again.
"Shags! Wake up. It's morning.
Time for breakfast."
Shags opened his eyes slowly.
He could hardly believe it.
He was in Sam's room.
And Sam was the same old
friend he'd always been.
He wasn't a giant anymore.

But what about the bone?

Shags raced out to the garden.
He dug as fast as he could.

And there it was, the same bite-sized
bone he had buried the night before!

Little Cat came purring over to play.
And Rabbit came hopping along.

For just a moment, Shags thought of
chasing Rabbit. But he changed his mind.

"Oh, no," he said to himself. "I'm never going
to chase anybody smaller than I am again!"